Disney

palace pets

Lily

Tiana's Helpful Kitten

For Nolan and Momo —T.R.

randomhousekids.com

ISBN 978-0-7364-3393-8 (trade)

Printed in the United States of America

10 9 8 7 6 5 4 3 2 1

Lily

Tiana's Helpful Kitten

By Tennant Redbank

Illustrated by Francesco Legramandi
& Gabriella Matta

Random House 🏠 New York

Lily's paws tapped to the music. The band was hot, hot, hot tonight!

Naveen played cool chords on his ukulele, while Louis's trumpet turned the heat up high. Tiana's Palace was the swingingest spot in all of New Orleans!

"Can you believe it, Lily?" Tiana asked. She brought her hands to her mouth

and watched the band. "I wanted this restaurant for so long. And now it's a big success!"

Lily purred. She wasn't surprised that Tiana's Palace was packed every night from dusk until dawn. Not with Tiana's incredible food and music like this!

Music was the very thing that had brought Lily and Tiana together. The sound of jazz had drawn Lily to Tiana's Palace. Tiana had seen the kitten by the door and welcomed her . . . into her restaurant, into her life, and into her heart.

Outside, the sky was getting lighter. It was almost dawn. The band played its last song.

"That is all, my friends," Naveen said when the final note faded. "We will see you tomorrow, yes?"

The guests clapped and hooted and whistled. Then, grabbing their hats and wraps, they trailed out of the restaurant.

Lily bounded onto the stage and over to the trumpet-playing alligator. "Louis, that was the bee's knees!" she said.

"Aw, shucks. It's nice to finally be playing with the big boys," Louis said. He rested his trumpet on the stage next to Lily.

Lily wrinkled her nose. The horn was stinky, tarnished, and dented. Her tail twitched with the urge to polish it.

"Want me to clean that for you?" she asked Louis, eager to help her friend.

"Nah, sugar," he said. "It smells like a swamp and sounds like a bayou. That's just the way I like it. I'd be lost without my scruffy ol' horn." He scratched his scaly skin and lumbered off.

Next to the stage, a window was open. A fresh breeze blew through it, ruffling Lily's fur.

"I'll just put his horn in the window to air out," she said.

She placed Louis's beat-up trumpet on

the windowsill. Then she leaped down to help Tiana with the cleanup.

Lily swept confetti from the floor. She picked up dropped napkins and silverware. She even found a single shoe behind one of the pillars. How could someone lose a shoe?

Tiana laughed when she saw Lily

with the lost shoe. She lifted Lily into the air.

"You're so good," Tiana said. "I wish people were as helpful as kittens."

Tiana rolled her eyes toward the corner of the stage and smiled. Naveen was curled up on a pile of dirty tablecloths, fast asleep.

Lily was tired, too. But she always felt better when she helped out. She just had to put Louis's trumpet away, and then she could nap.

She went back to the stage and jumped

onto the windowsill. She looked around, puzzled.

The windowsill was empty.

Louis's trumpet was gone!

Lily looked down. The horn had not fallen to the ground.

She looked to the left. Nothing.

She looked to the right. Down the street, she saw an old wagon pulled by a mule. That was just Samuel, the junk collector.

Junk collector?

Lily had an awful thought. What if Samuel had seen the trumpet on the windowsill? What if he had figured it was junk, left out for him?

Lily squeaked in alarm.

"Are you okay?" Lily's pony friend, Bayou, looked up at her from the stage.

"I've done something awful!" Lily said

in a rush. "I think I gave Louis's horn to the junk collector!"

"Louis's horn!" Bayou's eyes widened. "We have to get it back!" She backed up. "Watch out. I'm coming through!"

Lily stepped aside. Bayou took a running start, leaped, and soared through the open window. Her hooves just cleared the sill.

"Come on!" she called from the street. "Jump!"

Lily jumped! The moment her paws touched Bayou's back, the pony took off

after the junk wagon. They raced down the street. Bayou's hooves pounded the sidewalk.

"I think the wagon is slowing," Lily said in Bayou's ear. "Samuel must have a customer!"

Lily's eyes searched the junk cart. It was full of old items people didn't need anymore. Pots and pans. A rocking chair. Gas lamps and moth-eaten coats. Then Lily saw a hint of tarnished brass.

"Bayou!" she whispered. "There it is! The horn!"

Louis's horn sat on a pile in the junk cart, between a rag doll and a blue-and-white kettle. Lily frowned. How would she ever get it back?

"Excuse me, mister?" A little boy had approached Samuel. "Can I see that horn?"

Samuel pushed his hat back. "Sure, Henry," he said. He handed over the beat-up horn.

"I know that boy," Bayou whispered. "He hangs around the back door of Tiana's Palace and listens to the music."

Yes, Lily had seen him before, too. He liked music just as much as she did!

The boy cradled the horn in his hands. He raised it to his mouth and looked at Samuel. Samuel nodded. Then the boy began to play.

Lily tapped her paws and swayed.

Man, this kid was *good*! A small group of people gathered around the junk cart to listen.

Bayou whistled. "That's some talent," she said.

Lily nodded.

"How much?" Henry asked when he was done.

"Three dollars," Samuel told him.

The boy looked down at the trumpet. He handed it back. "Someday," he said a little sadly.

"*I'll* take it!" one of the men in the

crowd called. He peeled three bills from a fat roll of money.

Samuel raised an eyebrow at the kid. "Sorry, Henry," he said. "There will be other horns. I promise."

Samuel gave the horn to the rich man.

Lily blinked back tears.

It was so unfair! That trumpet was perfect for Henry. And the rich man? He had probably bought it just for kicks.

"Lily!" Bayou yelled. "That fellow has Louis's horn. We have to get it back!"

The rich man strolled down the street, swinging the horn and humming. Lily and Bayou followed him at a distance.

"Where's he going?" Lily asked.

The man turned into a tree-lined park with a fountain. He found a bench and sat down. He lifted the trumpet and looked at it closely.

"Well, here goes nothing," he said.

Putting the horn to his mouth, he puffed out his cheeks and blew.

BLAT!

Lily winced. Oof, that was awful!

Surprised, the man shook the horn, then tried again.

BLEAT! BLAT! BLAAAAAT!

"It sounds like a sick cow," Lily said.

Bayou swished her tail. "Make him stop!"

But the man didn't stop. *BLAT! BLEAT-A-BLAT BLAT BLAT!*

Lily put her paws over her ears. She loved music more than anything, but this? This wasn't music!

The man finally gave up. He glared at the horn. "What a piece of junk!" he said. "I need a real horn. Not an old rusty one. I know I can play just as good as anyone!"

He cocked his arm back and threw the trumpet as far as he could. It landed deep in a thicket.

Lily's eyes widened. The man had just thrown away Louis's horn! She dashed across the park. She reached the thicket and launched herself into the greenery.

Where is it? Where is it?

Lily rooted around in the bushes. The ground was muddy from rain. Her purple paws were turning brown. Still she kept going, until—

SCRITCH! Her claws raked against something hard. The trumpet!

Lily took the horn in her mouth and picked her way out of the bushes. Bayou was waiting for her.

"You found it!" Bayou cried.

Lily wanted to smile, but she couldn't. She had a trumpet in her mouth. She set the horn down on the ground.

"Phew!" she said. "I was starting to think we'd never get it back! The band just wouldn't be the same without Louis's trumpet."

Bayou tilted her head to one side. Her ears twitched. "Speaking of bands," she said, "do I hear music?"

Lily listened. Yes! It *was* music, and her favorite kind, too—jazz!

"We don't have to get back to Tiana's Palace just yet," Lily said. "Let's go listen."

Lily picked up the trumpet and followed Bayou across the park. A trio of musicians had set up by the fountain. People clustered around the band, dancing a two-step.

Lily craned her neck and balanced on her back paws. She could barely see. She was a tiny kitty, and there were a lot of people legs in her way.

A couple danced past, just missing her. They had almost two-stepped on her tail!

Lily hopped up onto the fountain. She felt safer with her tail off the ground. Plus she had a better view.

Oh, yeah! Lily started to sway. Music

was her favorite thing about New Orleans. She closed her eyes and let the beat fill her up. She could feel the jazz deep in her bones. She opened her mouth to purr—

Splash!

The trumpet fell out of her mouth and right into the fountain.

She watched it sink to the bottom.

Oh, no!

She'd lost Louis's trumpet . . . again!

The song ended. As the musicians began
a new one, they moved off across the park,
and the dancers followed. Lily and Bayou
were left behind.

Lily stared sadly at the trumpet.

Bayou poked her nose over the edge of
the fountain and shook her head.

"Do you think it's deep?" Lily asked

her. "I don't like getting my paws wet."

Bayou snorted. "I think more than just your paws are going to get wet," she said.

Lily sighed. Who knew that being helpful could be such trouble? She should have left Louis's trumpet alone.

Lily balanced on the edge of the fountain. She didn't want to lose the horn now. Still, she couldn't make herself jump in. "Maybe there's another way," she said. "Maybe I can— Oh!" Her paws slipped on the slick, wet marble. They slid out from under her and she tumbled backward—

tail over paws—right into the water!

She came up sputtering.

Bayou whinnied with laughter. "Well, that's another way, all right."

The water wasn't very deep. Lily took a breath and went under.

She looked around. A frog swam right in front of her! *How did he get in here?*

She shook her head and kept looking. *There!* The trumpet rested half a foot away. She picked it up with her mouth and lifted her head out of the water.

She'd done it!

Sopping wet, Lily pulled herself out of the fountain. She put the horn down and shook her fur. Water droplets flew in all directions.

Bayou reared. "Hey!" she cried. "You're getting me wet!" She shook her mane.

"Sorry!" Lily said. She smoothed out her soaking fur with her tongue. "I've learned my lesson. From now on, I'm not letting this trumpet out of my sight. We're taking it straight back to Louis!"

Lily jumped from the fountain. With the trumpet in her mouth, she and Bayou left the park.

Lily spotted a fish seller. She didn't stop to beg for scraps. She heard a fiddler. The music was lovely, but she turned away. She paused on a street corner just long enough to let a motorcar pass by.

Lily didn't notice the puddle in front of her. The big puddle. The muddy puddle.

The tires of the yellow motorcar rolled through the puddle.

Kersplash!

Mud splattered all over Lily and the

horn. Lily whimpered. *Why is everything going wrong today?*

"Ooh, I'm ever so sorry!" The owner of the car stopped and got out. She wrung her hands in despair. "I didn't see you there!"

The lady leaned in closer. She blinked. "Well, I declare! Lily, is that you?"

Lily looked up. The lady was Charlotte, Tiana's best friend!

"And my, oh my, it's Bayou, too!" Lottie went on. The pony and Lottie were good friends. Bayou lived in the stables at Lottie's big house.

"Oh, sweetie," Lottie said to Lily. "You

look like you've had an awfully rough day. Let me bring you back home and clean you up. I'll give you a nice bath and a brushing. You'll be as good as new! Then I'll take you to Tiana's Palace for the show tonight."

Lottie went to pick up Lily but stopped and wrinkled her nose. She bustled over to her car. "One moment!" she called. She unfolded a handkerchief and spread it over her leather seat.

"Hop in," she told Bayou. Bayou jumped into the back. Holding Lily at arm's length, Lottie deposited the wet, muddy kitten on the handkerchief.

After wiping her hands on another handkerchief, Lottie got into the car. "Y'all hold on now!" she yelled. Her foot stomped on the gas, and the motorcar squealed away.

Ten heart-thumping minutes later, the car pulled up to Lottie's house. Lottie was quite a fast driver!

Lottie took Lily inside and straight to the powder room. Lily still held the horn tightly between her teeth.

"Poor kitty," Lottie said. "You're just like Tiana. You work too hard! That girl doesn't know how to pamper herself."

She dropped Lily into a warm bubble bath. It felt lovely. Lily relaxed and let Lottie take the horn. There were no junk collectors there, or rich men, or thickets.

The horn was safe. Everything would be fine.

Lily purred as her fur was washed. She purred as her fur was dried. She purred as Lottie tied a big green bow around her neck. She felt good for the first time all day.

Maybe Lottie was right. Maybe she did work too hard. It was certainly nice to be treated like a princess!

"Now I have another surprise for you," Lottie told her. She clapped her hands and danced out of the room.

Lily tilted her head to one side. A surprise? What could it be? Maybe it was a crawfish treat. Maybe it was a big bowl of milk!

Lottie skipped back into the room, her hands behind her back.

"Ta-da!" she said. She pulled out a trumpet—a shiny, brassy, *new* trumpet.

"I had that nasty ol' horn all shined up for you," Lottie told Lily. "I even had the dents hammered out!"

Lily blinked . . . and fainted.

Lily opened her eyes. Lottie was standing over her, staring at her nervously. "Tiana's going to *kill* me," Lottie wailed. "I broke her kitten!"

Lily meowed.

"Oh! You're awake . . . and not broken!" Lottie dropped to her knees to cuddle her. Lily purred and let Lottie stroke her ears.

It wasn't Lottie's fault, after all. She had just been trying to help her friends. Lily knew what it was like to want to help the people she cared about . . . and to mess up.

Finally, Lottie calmed down. "I'm so glad you're okay," she told Lily. "Let me just get dressed. Then I'll drive us to Tiana's Palace."

Lily knew it would take Lottie a long time to get ready, so she went to the stables to tell Bayou what had happened. They looked at the horn. It was shiny and dent-free.

"Oh, Bayou," Lily said. "What am I going to do? Louis will be so mad! This horn doesn't smell like the swamp anymore. It smells like peaches and cream. I doubt it will ever sound the same again!"

"Just tell him the truth," Bayou said.

Lily sighed. Bayou was right, of course. But she could hardly breathe when she thought about confessing to Louis.

Way too soon, Lottie was dressed and ready to go. Lily secretly hoped for a long car ride, but they made it to Tiana's Palace in no time at all.

Lottie opened the car door for Lily, and she hopped down to the sidewalk. She followed Lottie into the restaurant.

Tiana greeted Lottie with a smile and a hug. "I'm so happy you came!" she said. Then she noticed Lily at her feet. "Lily!

I was wondering where you were! You've been working too hard. I'm glad you found time today to relax."

Relax? Lily's ears swung back. She had hardly relaxed. She thought about how she had raced down the street after the junk cart. Rooted through the thicket. Slipped into the fountain. Gotten splashed with mud. No, her day had hardly been relaxing. But she'd rather go through every one of those things again than face Louis.

Still, Lily held her head high. With

the shiny horn in her mouth, she weaved between the tables to get to the stage.

Louis was sitting on a stool in the corner. Lily hopped up next to him and placed the horn at his alligator feet.

"Louis," she confessed, "I lost your horn this morning. I got it back, but it's not the same. I don't think it sounds like the bayou anymore." She bowed her head. "I'm sorry. I was trying to be helpful, but all I did was mess up."

Louis picked up the horn. He turned it over and frowned.

"This shiny thing?" He laughed. "This isn't my horn. I've got my horn right here."

Louis reached into his bag and pulled out a tarnished and dented old trumpet.

Lily's eyes widened. She sniffed the horn. The trumpet smelled like the swamp. It was Louis's horn for sure!

"I—I don't understand," Lily said.

"Me neither," Louis said with a shrug. "When I left this morning, y'all were busy cleaning up. So I just grabbed my horn off the windowsill and skedaddled."

Lily sat down in shock. *Louis* had taken his horn? That meant the horn in Samuel's junk cart . . . it was just another horn. The horn she had searched the thicket for. The horn she had gone into the fountain for. Just another beat-up old horn. Not Louis's horn at all!

Louis held the trumpet up to the light and examined it closely. "Now, whatever are we going to do with this thing?" he asked.

Lily smiled. She still couldn't believe Louis had had his horn all along! "I think I have an idea," she said. She took the horn in her mouth and ran to the back door.

Sure enough, Henry was sitting on the step, waiting for the music to start. Lily dropped the horn at his feet.

Henry's face lit up. "For me?" he asked. His eyes never left the horn.

Lily meowed.

Henry raised the trumpet to his mouth and began to play. The music was cool and hot and wonderful. It was sweet, sweet jazz.

Oh, yeah. Lily's paws tapped. She swayed to the beat.

It was true—being helpful was hard work. Sometimes it didn't turn out the way you planned.

But sometimes, if you were lucky, it turned out even better!

Each Palace Pet has a

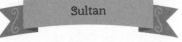
Sultan

Pumpkin

Berry

story to tell. Collect them all!

Petite

Treasure

Dreamy